MW00443341

Speaking your Truth is the most powerful tool we all have

-Oprah Winfrey

Published By Amazon

First Trade Paperback edition 2018

Copyright 2018 by Hareder McDowell

Amazon supports copyright. Copyright fuels creativity, encourages diverse voices, promotes free speech, and creates vibrant culture. Thank you for buying an authorized edition of this book and for complying with copyright laws by not reproducing, scanning, or disturbing any part of it in any form without permission. You are supporting the writers and allowing Amazon to continue to publish books for every reader.

Printed in the United States

ISBN 9781973588733

Book Design by Michael B. McDowell

Foreword

In the beginning, there was SEX. It pretty much drives all things: goods, services, meetings, dates, dinners, art, and film. Everything comes from or leads to sex. Crazy thing is even though sex is so natural and inevitable in various forms, many do not have an instruction manual for how you *do it*. Many parents assume the instructions for life and everything in it are passed down to children. The only issue with this belief is the author of said manual remains unknown, although you will likely pass down whatever your parents said or did to you.

Concerning sex, sometimes absolutely nothing is relayed through generations.

In the case of Black sex—yes, Black sex—a separate but equal manual is needed because this type of intimacy is shaped by racial and cultural constructs. Of course, the usual anatomical parts and organs are used for Black sex. What distinguishes Black sex from others is how this type of intimacy is taught.

Since Black women arrived in America, their bodies have been exploited throughout parts of history. Perhaps the darkest period is when the Black female body was used to reproduce en masse. Our offspring were and to some degree still are used to meet harsh labor and economic demands in the country. Early sex and pregnancy were encouraged because work had to get done.

Fast forward to the Reconstruction era. Black women are bound by the Bible. We were to wear long skirts and be something called "ladylike." Suddenly, we embraced a generation of committed wives and mothers who cared for families and outside children alike because maintaining a marriage was an accomplishment. The quality of the relationship was irrelevant. Sex was not for us. Sex was for men. You were taught to stay pure for your husband, then satisfy your husband; forsake all others until you die. Basically, you should never practice having sex, but you better be damn good at it after this ceremony where you give up your name, grab a ring, and jump a broom.

Now, jump to the civil rights movement, a time when so much unfolded around social and racial justice.

Orgasms, fidelity, and womanhood hardly topped concerns for Black people given the climate. Instead, Black women during this period were diligent, quiet, and faithful. They remained loyal to the cause, not to owning their sexuality. "Fast girls" and the "ones who appeared in magazines" did that. If you were not that type of woman, you would conversely skip talks about sex and use appropriate nicknames for your vaginal area, like "pocket book."

Fast forward to what looks like sexual freedom i.e 1970's. Pam Grier hit the big screen; fitted jeans are all the craze; Black women are sexier than ever. It seemed we reached a turning point for sexual liberation. This belief was superficial because few talked about sex. We created babies, raised babies, wed, and divorced. We still believed sex was reserved for girls in that other group—the "fast girls" and the "ones in magazines." No manual was written, yet sex was hardly discussed in our households.

Skip to the 1990s and early 2000s, when sultry girl groups with feminist undertones cropped up. Some sang in that crazy, sexy, and cool vibe. Others asked can you pay their bills or the liberated, spread-eagle hardcore rhymes of hip-hop. This must mean we are talking about sex, Black women have made it and according to the hypersexual love and whatever and housewives of whoever. This must mean Black women finally reached a place of freedom concerning their sexuality! right? Wrong. We just moved along. We survived but did not liberate.

Daily, young Black girls receive diagnoses caused by risky sex practices. Many of these girls became acquainted with sex in the same manner as their mothers and grandmothers. Everyone is watching and listening, but nobody is talking, really talking, about sex or the joy and pain that accompanies a sexual journey. These are a few stories taken from Black women and girls who through the good, bad, and evil figured it out.

Kim and Niecy

"Niecy, pick up the phone. Pick up the damn phone."

"Hello, Kim. You've been calling me all morning."

"I need your advice. You got three daughters. This my first one. Most shit I can handle or have an answer for, but I don't know what to say about this. I can't figure out why she would be doing something like this. Is she a freak or something? I don't get it, Kim."

"Calm down. Slow down, and tell me what the issue is."

"You know Tammy room is right across from mine, and we have the bathroom separating the rooms, right?"

"Kim, I've been to your house a hundred times. Why are you giving me the layout, stalling. Okay, Okay. I had to pee at like two, maybe two-thirty, in the morning. I hear something in Tammy room. The door is cracked, and I'm thinking she breathing heavy in her sleep. I look through the crack in the door, and you remember that huge teddy bear my brother won her at that amusement park for her eleventh birthday?"

"Yes, I remember the damn bear. Please get to the part that makes this an urgent call."

"Anyway, she was humping him."

"Excuse me, Kim."

"Niecy, you heard me. She was humping the bear. To be honest, she was liking the shit, like for real going full in on the bear. So I am calling you at 6 a.m. on a weekend because I have no idea how to face her when she wakes up. I mean, what do I say? What does this mean? Is she fucking already? Is she practicing?

Kim, be honest. When you were her age, you never did that, like to a pillow or anything?"

"No, I didn't. I shared a room with both of my sisters, and I don't think they was humping anything either.

Well, I did. I started early humping stuff on accident. When I realized what the finale of all that humping was, I got excited. Of course, I didn't know the term was orgasm. I knew when I did it, I wanted to hump something again. I didn't ask my mother about it, and I don't think she caught me. It's normal."

"I don't know, Niecy. I don't want to embarrass her, but I don't want to be in the dark about her feelings. That makes me nervous. Should I say something?"

"I think you should just bring it up while y'all watching something that has a kissing scene or something."

"And say what, Niecy? 'Do you do stuff like this to your teddy bear at night?'"

"No, Kim. I mean use it as a chance to spark the awkward conversation, or maybe get a book on masturbation. Leave it on her bed."

"Masturbation! Girl, didn't nobody talk to us about no damn masturbation. I mean my uncles would crack jokes when my little brother started having wet dreams and jacking off, but that was their thing. Like it was a rite of passage or something to start beating-ya-meat.

But me and my sisters, no. There was no talk about, 'hey, it's ok to play with yourself.' I mean, is it ok?"

"Is what ok, Kim?"

"Playing with yourself? It's ok now. Like I love my magic bullet. I don't leave home without it, but eleven is too young to be encouraging that."

"Are you encouraging it if she already does it?"

"I mean why do we use the bullet and all these other toys now?"

"Niecy, you know I use them so I don't answer them 'u up' text messages from Chris bum ass."

"What would happen if you didn't use it?"

"I would end up over there, up under him and pissed in the morning."

"Exactly, so playing with yourself helps you save yourself from regret sex. Right, Kim?"

"Yeah, but I'm grown, and I know what I'm doing."

"How long did it take you to know what you doing?"

"I guess after high school or after her dad. I don't know. Bottom line is I use my toys and masturbation to calm myself. 'Cause when I am horny I don't think, not rationally at least. It's almost like a high. I need to come down, so I can keep it moving."

"Kim, that makes perfect sense. I do the same thing. What if we learned thatat eleven?"

Conversation Starters for Kim and Neicy?

1. Was masturbation discussed with you in your household?
2. Do you agree masturbation is a prevention method to help avoid sexual decisions?
3. At what age is a talk about masturbation is necessary?
4. Is there a double standard on masturbation among men versus women?

Beverly and Andrea

"Andrea, get down here, and eat this food before it gets cold."

"I'm coming, Mama."

"And change that radio station. You know we don't listen to that trash in this house."

"Sorry, Mama."

"Change that shirt. You not wearing that to church. I don't know where you got them big ol' breast from, not from my side of the family for sure. You need something loose. Women of God don't show all of that. They don't go out in this world tempting these men. You got your lap scarf? I can see your knees in that skirt. I don't want nobody thinking we raising no Jezebel."

"Yes, mama. I have my scarf, and I'll change my shirt. I'm sorry."

"You should be, Drea. You know better. Come back down and eat after you change. We need to leave for choir rehearsal."

"Mama, did daddy come in this morning?"

"He didn't make it back. You know his work keeps him long. He is a pastor. A lot of people need him; the sick and shut-in need they pastor. They call him all the time, and we support him. Don't look like that while you asking me, 'did he come in?'"

"But, Mama, this like the fifth day. We see him when we at the church, but he always gotta be something to somebody. We didn't even do nothing on

Mother's Day after the second service like he promised you."

"Look, I married a man of God, and I knew what I signed up for. Stop asking me all this. Eat your food."

"But what does he do that takes overnight? Mama, don't get offended, but my friend Keiana from school, her dad is a councilman, you remember?"

"Yeah, I remember her."

"Well, he was always gone at first for the campaign. Then after he won, he had these meetings and trips and policy stuff, I guess. They found out last week he got his assistant pregnant. Now Keiana is about to have a little brother or sister. But I'm thinking why don't she leave? He cheated. That's a sin, right? So she supposed to leave him, right, Ma?"

"What does this have to do with your father and I, Andrea?

"He always gone to. Are we gone stay if he get somebody pregnant?"

"Don't go comparing your father to any other man. I don't know Keiana and her family business, but her mother is right for upholding the word of God and standing by her husband and staying in that marriage.

Keiana's dad has done a lot for this community. We don't have many Black men in politics working for the good of our people. Women always tempting married men—especially men in power—trying to break up their family. We are lucky to be blessed with good husbands who give us good homes and take care of their families. No, we don't quit on them when they make a mistake.

You don't just give your husband away because his flesh got weak."

"Mama, does your flesh get weak?"

"Hebrews 13:4: 'Marriage should be honored by all, and the marriage bed kept pure. For God will judge the adulterer and all the sexually immoral.' Now eat your food!"

Conversation Starters for Beverly & Andrea

1. Is infidelity forgiven when men are powerful public figures versus when they have no clout?
2. Was the scripture an answer to Andrea's question about her mother's flesh getting weak?
3. What lesson is Beverly teaching her daughter about marriage?
4. Do you agree that when women tempt married men, the men are tempted into infidelity?

Lisa and Dana

"Great game today, baby girl. Y'all were so cute in your cheerleading uniforms and when y'all did all those little tricks and flips. I remember the day I could move like that."

"Ma, you could move like this? Lil' Miss Dana, don't get it twisted. That's how I got your daddy back when I was in high school."

"Yeah, ok. That was thirty years ago!"

"Same rules apply, little girl. But enough about me and your daddy. Who is that little boy you was blushing at the whole time. What they call that in the movie, *Bring it on*, cheer sex?

"Ma, stop being a creep!"

"Do you like him? Y'all go together? Do they still say that, 'go together?'"

"Kind of. Like he plays ball. I'm a cheerleader. It's goals for real."

"Goals. Y'all kids kill me with that. Is he a senior too?"

"Yeah, he a senior. He got accepted to Hampton just like me. We been talking about it a lot."

"What happened to your boyfriend that stayed down the street? What's his name, Earl?

"Ma, I haven't talked to Earl in months. I just kind of get bored. He at another school. It's too much. I guess my mind changes."

"Your mind changes, Dana, about boyfriends?

"Yes, kind of. I'm figuring out my type, I guess."

"Dana, be careful with that figuring out mess. I met your father in high school. We started dating, went to college together, got married after college, and had you and your sister. If we would've gotten bored or tired of each other, you wouldn't be here."

"I understand, Ma. I mean, that's a true love story, I guess. But you always tell me to have options. You made me apply to ten schools, and we went on tours to make the right choice. You made me take ballet, tap, even had me praise dancing before we settled on cheer. You even force me to try new food when you know I can live off chicken and cheese."

"Dana, what's your point?"

"Why can't I do the same thing with boyfriends. I mean, you tried one and signed up for forever."

"That's different. You can't go exploring your options with people like food and schools."

"But, Ma, both of those are important to your entire life, right? I mean how do you know that dad is the best you could have ever had, I mean, what does he compare to?"

"I fell in love with him and never needed to know there was another option. He has always been enough for me."

"Mom, what is enough and how do you know? Somebody who has been starving for a day will think bread and milk is enough but not somebody who is accustomed to a buffet. You know the rest. These are your words, mom, not mine!"

"I know what I said, little girl, but that doesn't apply to women. We live in a world that sets double standards and women who go around exploring all of their options get reputations that they can't get rid of. People start thinking they are loose and start calling them hos."

"You understand?"

"I do, and I don't. I can't explore my options in men or have sex with them."

"Dana, I ain't say nothing about sex! You having sex?"

"Ma, stay focused."

"I can't explore my options because I will be ho, or people will think I am a ho. I have to take my chance and marry a man at some point that is ok with my clean reputation, but his reputation doesn't have to be clean. He basically picks me because I am good enough? Is that what you're saying?"

"I am saying that you can't be out here loose, just having sex with a bunch of men. No man will want to marry you because so many men have been with you."

"So, stay a virgin until I get married, or are you saying five guys is a good number? Like how many make you a ho?"

"You killing me! Dana, I'm saying that you don't want to be used up. If I had to put a number on it, I would tell you what my mama told me. Don't have sex with more men, than fingers you have."

"Ma, that's ten—ten men—in my entire life?"

"Dana, you think it should be more?"

"I'm just thinking how am I supposed to prepare for this number. I mean I had one boyfriend in high school. I like this boy now, and I'm going to college in the fall. I'll probably like somebody there. That's three. I'm only eighteen. If I don't like him all four years and explore one or two more options, I'll be at five. I graduate at twenty-two. If I don't secure a potential husband by then, I'll only have five more men to sleep with before my mid-twenties because after that I'll be a ho and nobody will want me. Is that what you're saying, Ma?"

"Yes!"

"I don't think that's fair. Men get however many they want. When they find a wife, they are pretty experienced with women and our bodies because they had practice, but we don't have nobody to practice with to be ready for them."

"That's the way of the world, baby girl. I didn't create it I just live in it."

"So if he is experienced and you are inexperienced, don't that make things kind of boring or kind of off? I mean, what do we call women that are more experienced?

"Side chicks."

Conversation Starters for Lisa and Dana

1. What number of partners makes you a wife, and what number of partners makes you a ho?
2. What does Lisa mean by, "Side Chicks"?
3. What will you teach a young woman regarding the connection between sex partners and her reputation?

Tisha and Daisy

"Tisha, let me explain something to you. Pussy is a good for a service. They get what they pay for!"

"Ma, you crazy. If I like him, I like him, right? Don't that count?"

"Don't be no fool, baby girl. That one bedroom we lived in, the endless bus cards, and food stamps, remember that?"

"Yeah, Ma. What does that have to do with me liking David?"

"That's what 'like' got me with your daddy. I really, really liked your daddy. His entire broke ass had me in love, in like, and in stupid."

"Mama, you always talk about how much you loved daddy and how you all hung out and watched your favorite shows and cooked for one another. That wasn't enough?"

"Of course, we watched our favorite shows, without cable, and ate whatever we could piece together. The only good thing I got out of it was you. Bottom line, if I would have known what I know now, I would already be on my first Birkin, instead of my first Céline. I am trying to school you before you get to liking people and giving away that precious tool and treasure."

"Tool and treasure, Ma?"

"Yep, it's a tool, a powerful tool that has literally started wars and made the strongest the weakest. Your grandmother used to say that."

"Daisy, that thing is the carriage of currency. As long as it works, you don't have to! I didn't listen, and you better make sure you do."

"What did you do, Mom, if like and love doesn't matter?"

"Listen, baby, you have to love yourself enough to know you are worth the best of things, the best of everything, and your most prized possession is that one thing all men crave. You have to prey on their craving. It's uncontrollable and most of them lose all access to the brains in their heads when they are thinking about you."

"Mama, how do you know this, to use this and that and prey and what not?"

"While I was waiting on the bus stop, messing around with yo damn daddy, a guy pulled up to the light in a black Benz and told me I was too sexy to be on the bus stop. I didn't think so. I blushed and tried to ignore him. He pulled around and asked where I was going and offered me a ride. I was nervous at first because I thought he was a drug dealer or maybe a crazy man, but I took a chance.

He dropped me off at the mall I worked in at the time and told me to call him. The entire ride I'm looking at his watch, his phone, even having a cell phone was fancy back then. His face-off radio, just everything. I was in awe, basically. Once I got off work, I couldn't stop thinking about him. I got off work, missed my bus, was late getting you from day care. I was rushed and tired. All I remember is walking in the door to your daddy who had warmed up some noodles and made me a grilled cheese. It pissed me off. After that one ride, I was thinking, 'I'm too good for this.'

As soon as I got the chance, I made that call. He met me on the bus stop the next day. While on the way to work, he asked if I was hungry.

I said, 'yes.'

He asked me what I wanted. I said, 'I don't know. It don't matter,' thinking I'm being polite.

Then, he told me in the deepest, sexiest, most secure voice, 'you can have anything you want.'

I was hooked, I was so use to your daddy telling me, 'you can order from this side of the dollar menu, or no, you can't get cheese on that.'

I didn't know what to do. That night he picked me up from work and as we pulled up. He asked me to kiss him. I knew I was right in front of the house, but I felt like he bought me lunch. He deserves a kiss.

By the end of that week, it had become a common thing for me to see Quincy in the Benz, rolling by the bus stop and through the mall parking lot. One Thursday, he stopped in my store, a retail chain, that sold perfume. He asked me what my favorite perfume was, and I gave him a random answer because my perfume was a mixture of ramen seasoning and soap. He picked it up, and bought it for me. I was so in awe that it was so easy for him to buy me such an expensive perfume. Well, $40 was expensive to me at the time. Of course, he picked me up that night and asked if he could smell the perfume on me. I felt like he bought me the perfume, so he deserves a smell. He took the bottle and sprayed it on my chest, laid his head on my breast, and inhaled. As he was smelling, he ran his fingers through my hair, and the link on his watch got stuck. I had been wearing the same ponytail for weeks, meaning to do something to my hair, but never got around to it. It was matted and nappy.

I looked up at him and said, 'I need money to get my hair done.'

I felt so crazy and uncomfortable until he pulled the cash out of his pocket and gave it to me. After that, he reached into my blouse with one hand and unbuttoned my jeans with the other. He had driven me to and from work and bought me food and perfume. Now he gave me cash for my hair. He deserved to feel me."

"Ok, Ma. I hear all of that, but how did he make you feel. What did he look like?"

"Doesn't matter, Tisha. What mattered was that he knew what he was paying for, and I knew in that moment I had something worth paying for. I never saw your dad the same after that. Love and like drifted. I loved living well. You do too. Quincy gave me the confidence to go from asking for hair, food, shoes, and bags to cars and homes. Nothing is free, especially me."

"Mama, I wouldn't know where to start with asking men for anything."

"Start small, baby girl. Hold on to it until you have what you want. Make that the expectation. Save love and like for your family. Everybody else pays for it."

"I hear you, mama. No freebies, and I should be able to get whatever I want if I am giving them what they want."

"Exactly, Tisha. It's an arrangement that was understood since the beginning of time. Let men be men, and let them take care of you. Don't fuss as long as you are paid for. Don't complain. Don't question."

"Too bad for David then. I guess I really liked him."

"Yes, too bad for him. Now, go pick up your damn daddy. He wants to see you. The bus don't come this far north."

<u>Conversation Starters for Tisha and Daisy</u>

1. Do you agree you should be compensated in some way if you have sex with a man?
2. Does wealth and lifestyle truly affect a relationship?
3. Do you agree with the mother in this story? Why, or why not?

Pricilla and Jamie

"The reality of every situation is every man will cheat on you. No one gets 100 percent of nothing."

"Mother and her love philosophy, she making me hate my boyfriend before I even get him. Damn! Just because she on her third husband and the first two cheated, don't mean that's my story, right?"

"Jamie, come downstairs. Your Mama wants to talk to you."

"Here I come, Mama."

"Tell mama about that lil boy who dropped you off yesterday. Oh my God, is that why you screamed for me to come down here?

"Yes, it is. High school is where the relationship foolishness starts, all that mess about going together.

Where the hell you going?"

"Stop laughing, Mama. Don't nobody even say 'go together' no more!"

"Well, whatever you doing, make sure your options are open. You been with that boy since you were in eighth grade, and you're a senior. You too young to be serious."

"What you mean my options? You're encouraging me to have multiple boyfriends?"

"Yes! I absolutely am! Everybody needs multiple everything, especially a teenage girl. High school is the first layer of devastation, with a lifetime of devastation to come if all your eggs are in one basket and all your attention is focused on one person."

"Isn't that love, someone having all of your attention?"

"Absolutely not, girl! Anybody having all of anything means they can take it all away. Never forget that."

"What are you saying?"

"Jamie, you can like whoever you want, even fall in love. The person you should be the most in love with is yourself. Give 50 percent to yourself. Spread the other 50 percent among family and men, as you see fit. You see, women give over 100 percent of themselves to everything, leaving nothing for themselves. Have you ever seen an older couple where the man looks good—aged well, has great teeth, is well-groomed, and doesn't seem to have a lot of weight gain? Then you glance at his wife. She looks like 'the hired help.'"

"Ma, I hate to admit it, but I have."

"Exactly, she gave over 100 percent to him and probably their kids; meanwhile, he maintained his happiness, which is reflected in how well he aged. I'm not saying don't love. I'm not saying to get married. I am saying always keep your options open. Dance a little. Flirt a little. Allow your ego to be stroked. If you want to go further, go further. It's your one life to live. I know you judge me for my divorces and dating, but I have lived a happy life. When I was unhappy, I was done. Each time I left one, I was happier than the last. The cheating did piss me off, but I was not devastated."

"What's the difference?"

"Honey, devastated is when you find out he was cheating, and you go into a rage that converts into sadness and depression then transitions into bitter. Bitter is like a shit-coated, honey-bun glaze that covers your next relationship. I didn't go into either phase because I had options. There was always another plan or another card to play that gave me security and satisfaction."

"Why bother, mom? Why commit? Why marry?"

"To try, honey. To pledge your allegiance to someone until you can't anymore. It might last a lifetime. It might not. In the meantime, do what makes you happy to avoid looking like 'the help'!"

Conversation Starters for Priscilla & Jamie

1. What are your thoughts on this quote from Priscilla: "Anybody having all of anything means they can take it all away"?
2. Have you met a couple where the wife looked like "the help"?
3. Do you agree a woman should always have options?

Rita and Debra

"Rita, hand me my glass and come roll my hair for me."

"What you getting all fresh for tonight, Ms. Deb."

"I'm headed out to go stepping with a guy from the job."

"Rita, you been quiet and weird the last couple days. What's going on with you?"

"I just having been feeling stress or something."

"Rita, what kind of stress does a fifteen-year-old have?"

"Hand me another roller, Ma."

"Answer the question, Rita."

"I'm pregnant. It's Mike's baby."

"Mike, the basketball player at the high school?"

"Yeah, him."

"Didn't I drop you off over there one time for a birthday party or something?"

"You did. What's the point?"

"That was his family's home, that big Greystone building?"

"Yeah, Ma. That's where he live. You met him too."

"Hmmm, what year is he, a senior?

"Ok, what he say his next move is?

"He got a basketball scholarship to one of those big ten schools. It's a big deal, I guess."

"You keeping it!"

"What, Ma?"

"Rita, I am telling you. You keeping it. When you grandmother got pregnant with me, my daddy was married and owned a lounge. She ended up with this house we living in now, and he had to pay monthly to keep things neat, you know?"

"Yeah, so what does that have to do with me?"

"Let me finish, girl! Then I got pregnant with you when I was sixteen. Your daddy was a barber then, but I knew he was gone own a shop one day. I secured my spot early. I mean, yeah, he like ten years older than me, and I knew I would be straight if I had his baby. Basically, everything I been able to do for you, getting pregnant by him set me up for it."

"Ma, what you're saying is that I need to keep this baby? I'm a junior in high school. I don't know nothing about being a mom."

"Rita you'll be aight. First thing you need to do is make sure that's his baby. Don't tell him until you too far along for an abortion. Keep hanging with him, though. He probably got the type of mama that's gone get lawyers and run tests, but we gone do that first. When you start showing, we gone go down to the state office and get you signed up for a voucher. The state will probably give you about $1,000 to rent a place, and we can move out of here, finally. They probably will give you stamps.

"Ma, you going in, ain't you? It's like you excited or something."

"Look, as of yesterday I didn't know what your future looked like. Today, we planning. You got a baby by a basketball player who is going to school on scholarship. You a basketball-player-baby -mama, better than a married man, better than a barber. You the next generation, baby."

"Wow, Ma. I never thought about it like that."

"I know. Put my scarf on, so I can sit under this dryer."

"Ma, what you think I'm having?"

"A daughter!"

Conversation Starters for Rita & Debra

1. Is this a realistic conversation, and do you know of any situations where this has been taught?
2. If the prospect of financial stability and security is based on having a baby, should that leverage the choice in keeping a pregnancy.
3. How can we address teen pregnancy from a non-judgmental stance?

<u>Karen & Tina</u>

"Where you coming from, Tina?"

"Mama, I don't even want to say. I'm so discouraged or better yet, defeated. I've accomplished everything I have set out to do, school, degrees property, a husband, dream wedding, great friends, great career, and now this. This I just can't seem to do."

"Baby, I don't understand. That kind of thing doesn't run in our family at all. Never have. If anything, we had too many never planned and never even wanted. I don't know what to say. Stay in prayer. God will deliver in time."

"I hear you, Ma. I just can't see my future as complete without it. I just have to switch up my lifestyle, I suppose. I know, I was an athlete in high school. That made everything irregular. Then I gained weight. That was from all the different prescriptions I was on, thinking it was prevention. I feel like every time I saw a new commercial for one thing, there was a law firm asking you to call and add yourself to a class-action suit for another product I thought worked. I really have no idea what I was on all through high school and college. Clearly, that caused some issues now."

"Tina, I don't know how to make sense of this. I was hard on you and probably threatened to put you out at the thought. I was fearful of how your life would change and become harder and how people would look at you and judge for being that young."

"Mom, I feel like I'm being punished. If it's not one vitamin, it's another. If it's not one family member asking, it's the next. I'm working out. I'm praying and meditating. It is at the top of my vision board. I'm loving and loyal to my husband. I'm successful. This I don't have the answer to. I wish people would stop asking. Mom, I wish you would stop asking."

"Asking what, baby?"

"For a grandchild!"

Conversation starters for Karen & Tina

1. Are there infertility support systems among African-American women?
2. Is success directly linked to the ability to become a mother?
3. Is it rude to ask when someone is having a baby?
4. In the medical industry, are you encouraged to have children at a certain age?
5. How do we teach young women how to plan a pregnancy?

Nana and Trisha

"Who is Cadi B?"

"Nana, you mean, Cardi B. What you doing asking me about her? What you been listening to?"

"That award show you had me watching, they say she rich now from making all that noise. I can't believe that's music to y'all, but I can't fuss 'cause my mama ain't think the G-funk All-Stars was singing music neither. I damn sho' couldn't explain Rick James, so whatever. To each generation its own."

"Dang, Nana, I appreciate the open mind. I just knew you was about to go in on Cardi B."

"Go in where?"

"It's a saying, Nana, like complain about or to talk about her."

"Oh, girl, don't take me too far. I'm trying to understand."

"I hear you, Nana. What else you like about our generation?"

"Y'all so free. I don't agree with a lot of it, but I guess I don't understand it all."

"What you mean, Nana?"

"Y'all wear different-color hair and don't care about all that cussing. Your clothes so damn tight, legs and ass everywhere all the time. Y'all yelling at the men on all the television shows, just seem like y'all don't care. You just live. Y'all put everything in that phone up on the computer too."

"I understand what you saying, Nana. I guess we just do whatever we want to do and wear whatever we want, unapologetically. We create, talk back, and make our own money. Yeah, that's free. Yeah, we post a lot too. Social media matters, Nana. Likes and retweets are major factors in everything."

"See that's what I don't understand. Why does everyone have to know everything and every move and see every thigh and every boob?"

"Nana, you rhyming!"

"I'm making a point, Trisha."

"I hear you. I just think your generation was quiet and polite."

"No, we were ladies and private, Trish."

"What does that even mean, a lady?"

"We kept things to ourselves, in our house and in our pants. Stuff was our business."

"I get that, Nana, but you raised me to speak up and be fearless. I know your generation had to be quiet and ladylike. You kept your business in the house, but that's not always freedom.

Your generation was classic. Knee length skirts, pin curls, hosiery, heels— just put together. When you show old footage of marches and protests, I always think that looks like a lot of work to do in a skirt."

"Trish, it was hard, but we maintained the reputation of Black women. At that time, we couldn't afford to be judged and ridiculed for what we wore or how we spoke. We were trying to move the entire race forward and raise families."

"We appreciate it, Nana. We scream because you all sacrificed your voices. We scream by speaking, singing, and rapping about what concerns us with no regard to who is judging or ridiculing us. We scream when we wear what we want, show our bodies when we want, and love who we want. We are still marching but in whatever we feel like marching in, Nana."

"It's just so much and hard to understand at times. I'm trying, though. I don't know. You all just so free. If we don't try to understand and talk to y'all, we will get offended. We so protective. The last thing we want is you all getting hurt from being judged and ridiculed."

"No way to be Black in this country without judgment, ridicule, and hurt. You taught me that, Nana. Y'all raised us to be able to handle it."

"Well, I guess so. Y'all just move without care even though white folks, men, and other countries judge."

"Nana, you forgot our biggest judge."

"Who?"

"Black Women."

Conversation Starters for Nana and Trisha

1. What music or movies from your generation did your grandmother not understand?
2. Why is it important to understand and engage with what is trending in the current generation?
3. How can we teach elders to be more understanding of the current generation?

Bri & Karen

"I didn't not want to raise you. You were taken from me."

"Taken! Don't try to blame the one mother I know for you not wanting to take responsibility for your own child."

"Look Bri, I'm not trying to taint your vision of your grandmother, but you twenty-two. I'm finally ready to at least start to mend what's supposed to be a mother-daughter relationship. I get it's late, but I was a confused child. Your grandmother was aggressive. I did as I was told."

"Don't 'look Bri' me, thinking I'm supposed to just understand or forgive, Karen. It ain't that sweet."

"Just listen for a min. I was in high school. I had been attracted to women since I don't know, fourth maybe fifth grade. I knew what I felt when I saw Whitney Houston or Jasmine Guy on TV. The feeling wasn't that of a regular fan. It was a real attraction. Your grandmother picked up on it just like everything else.

I remember watching, *A Different World*, and it was the episode where Jada Pinkett was in the new class. I just had this look like, 'who the hell is that?' In that moment, my mama was watching my face and looked disgusted.

Now, I had never actually been with a woman at that point. I didn't know what I was feeling or what I wanted to do, but she clearly did. She was dead set on fixing me. After months of Bible thumping, letting me know I was going against God, that my feelings were unnatural, constantly dressing me up in pink dresses, Barbie, and cheerleading this and that, I begin to think I liked men.

At freshman year in high school, I was encouraged to have sex with a man. This was to ensure my heterosexuality. Homecoming was coming up. I had to have a date—a male. Tim, your dad, was in the tenth grade and cool. Mama liked him. It seemed only right to make him my date. That night, I slept with Tim.

It was the worse experience of my life. It was fully consensual sex with words, but my body and my mind was repulsed. I laid there, just taking it and thinking that this was not what I wanted.

A month later, I came out to everyone. I switched up my look to be more comfortable. I quit the cheerleading team and finally began to truly love and learn myself. I was asked to leave the church and choose between my home and my sexuality."

"What you mean choose?"

"Get out, or don't be gay. That was my ultimatum until we found out I was pregnant with you. Mama looked at me with love again because she was excited to not only have a grandchild but also another girl. After you were born, she was able to focus on you and let me live.

When I went away to school, I never planned on coming back. I packed my trunk and headed to Florida A&M. Her last words were, 'I won't mess up with this one.'"

"Well, she did mess up. Last thing I need is a Lesbian mama!"

<u>Conversation Starters for Bri & Karen</u>

1. Is this a realistic story within the community you are familiar with?
2. Do you believe your biases and phobias have an influence on your younger female relatives?
3. Did the matriarchs in your family impact you? How so? What, if anything, have you changed?
4. What is your knowledge on sexual identity and identifying in early adolescence?

Acknowledgement

The best thing about being raised by Black women is being given the tools and methods for survival by any means. These stories are a culmination of survival stories surrounding the wonderfully complicated world of sex. As a sexologist and community psychologist, I talked with Black women near and far. I thank them for telling their stories for the sake of advanced research. I must acknowledge my mother and grandmother for always providing a sexually free platform that opened doors for my own sexual liberation. This liberation led to the ultimate blessing, my husband, my support, and friend. To every little Black girl who I have had the pleasure of working with and teaching, thank you. You are why I work.

Made in the USA
Monee, IL
25 January 2022

89734481R00042